Carmilla

A Dark Fugue

Also by David Brian

Dark Albion

Carmilla: The Wolves of Styria

The Cthulhu Child

Kaleen Rae: And Other Weird Tales

Carmilla

A Dark Fugue

David Brian

Night-Flyer

Carmilla: A Dark Fugue

2013 David Brian

2013 Night-Flyer Publishing

The right of David Brian to be identified as the author of this work has been asserted by him in accordance with the Copyright, Designs and Patents Act 1988.

All rights reserved. No part of this publication may be reproduced, stored in or introduced to a retrieval system, or transmitted, in any form, or by any means (electronic, mechanical, photocopying, recording or otherwise) without the prior written permission of the copyright owner, except for brief quotation in reviews. Any person who does any unauthorized act in relation to this publication may be liable to criminal prosecution and civil claims for damages. This book is a work of fiction which contains characters created by Joseph Sheridan Le Fanu and David Brian.

ISBN-13: 978-1492836490

ISBN-10: 1492836494

First published in 2013 by Night-Flyer Publishing

Dedication

For my Mum, who is the best at what she does

and does everything with a kind heart.

With a special word of thanks to Phillip and Jackie Cooper

who, with keen eyes and endless patience,

helped put all of this together.

Chapter 1

Excerpt from the private journal of Thomas Bennett. *September 11th, 1860.*

I have spent long hours pondering the facts revealed to me these past days, it is a truth only fully realised by the discovery of my *old friend's* journal. Strange then, that even after all which has occurred, and even in light of these further revelations, I still refer to him as *friend*.

Certainly his hands are stained crimson, and I knew this already, but such deeds as these he has undertaken, did I ever truly know the man?

Even now as I stare at the *weathered* pages of his journal, which now lays open on my desk, placed carefully alongside my own. I wonder, did he choose to abandon the book, that the crimes contained within be better understood, or did the necessity of circumstance force uncharacteristic haste?

So many questions remain as a result of these recent horrors, and it is likely I shall never attain all the answers I would seek;

however, there is one thing which does remain most likely. Should the church elders in Gratz, or the gendarmerie learn of the General's discarded tome, then they will almost certainly seek to claim it. I sense there is a wish on their part to remove these occurrences from history, but too many wives and daughters have already been lost, and as a father myself, how could I be complicit with such a deceit?

I have therefore taken the conscious decision to transcribe the most relevant of these events onto the pages of my own journal. It is important the world remains steadfastly aware, for Satan's minions move freely amongst us, as we in Styria have discovered to our recent great cost.

My *friend's* words present as an affront to my senses, jarring at my soul, and reaching out to me from the *yellowed* pages of his book. However, I must move past my own scorn of this man, as it is, I feel, imperative I set down *his* account of the events which unfolded.

The book before me rests open on pages dated *June 29th* in this year of our Lord *1860.*

Chapter 2

Excerpt from the journal of General Spielsdorf, *June 29th, 1860*

The date was June 28th in the year of our Lord 1860, and I knew the success of this night would depend on my keeping a clear head, and yet throughout our journey I had remained in distraction. The affliction of a recent loss does not readily allow one's mind to settle.

"We must be getting close now, Soldier Brother." Rudolph's words finally sharpened my senses, although it was partly the disdain I felt for his choice of reference which gave edge to my wit. The actions I have witnessed these past days can afford me little grace, and serve to instil nothing but contempt for all *seven* of my *brothers*.

Ever though, I am mindful, ours remains a righteous cause. Still, even with God on our side, I remain deeply troubled.

We eight had, for some time, been moving steadily through an expanse of open country. The horses had been restricted to a slow gait, as even beneath the light of a half-moon, and on a land which remained flat and uninteresting, a broken leg could still prove likely for such ungainly creatures. All about us lay fields of negligently cultivated land, broken hedges and fences in disrepair.

Finally though, we came to a point before us which extended into freshly cultivated tracts, and these fields were bordered on the western side by white-sand-hills. Away in the distance, at the far side of these laboured lands, stretched the sylvan confines of an immense pine forest.

"This is it," nodded Rudolph, and from there insisted that the horses be abandoned. We tied them securely at the forest border, allowing enough slack for the beasts to graze, and proceeded on foot.

I, after checking my pistol and sword, moved forward into the bleakness of the forest, a lantern held before me. None of my *brothers* carried torches, and they moved as phantasms, appearing then fading into the darkness before me.

Under the lantern's glare the forest presented an array of imagined threats, an opaque army of fiends, silhouettes which danced and swayed menacingly about us as we pushed on through the woodland. The poor light and dense growth combined to present an almost impervious covert tract, which for me proved a most wretched journey; my *brothers* moved with unhindered ease.

Felix had, at the point from where we discarded the horses, been sent ahead to scout our quarry, and though we had been in the forest for what seemed an age, as yet he had failed to return.

I turned to Rudolph, a question on my lips, "Do you think all remains well with Felix?"

Even amongst the semi-darkness of the pines I could see Rudolph's cold yellow eyes burning into me. A tone of distain scratched his voice as he replied, "Felix, I am sure, remains untroubled, Soldier Brother. These fiends are as nothing to us."

I made no reply, choosing instead to proceed on in silence, though once again I found myself questioning this unholy alliance. It is a thing I have done often since we left the hinterlands.

I and my father before me, and his father before him, every one of us a soldier born. I descend through a lineage lined with men of honour, so how is it then I am so easily able to align myself to these *people?* I am now in life's middle years, and yet here I find myself, hunting revenants, un-dead monsters that prey on the innocent. Yet these *men* with whom I share my quest, their faces wear open masks of satisfaction, relishing each and every act of ferocity and violence committed. These are *people* who rejoice in the viciousness of their hunt, the finality of their kill. These are *men* of hate!

At a point in the forest where we reached a large clearing, centred by a lone, monolithic English Yew, we turned in an easterly direction, in line with the instructions I had received earlier.

The previous morning I had ventured to an inn, in the village of Per. I travelled alone, as I sought information and as previously stated my companions are fearsome looking men, and thus poorly equipped for engaging *locals* in idle chatter, especially when doing so with a view to garnering knowledge.

My conversation was restricted to the innkeeper whose name was Antonio Russo, and, as his name suggests, was born of Italian stock. Also, a wiry, white haired old man named Leo, who supported himself with a gnarly old cane, which was as twisted as the fellow's defected spine.

I introduced myself as a passing traveller, and made general comments with regard to their local community, although truthfully my ears were only attentive for matters of a certain nature.

I had endeared myself to the *keep* by purchasing the solitary bottle of wine he retained on his shelf, although the bitter assault of the *dry white* upon my palate suggested I would have been better served with ale.

Eventually though, the conversation turned in the direction I sought.

The bar-keep told me of a German family, who had moved to the area several years earlier. The Krauss family were paupers, but had taken advantage of the ancient forest laws, and beneath its applied protection had constructed for themselves a modest habitation. In the proceeding years, Hans Krauss had proven himself to be a hard working individual, who ostensibly applied himself as a woodcutter amid the sylvan vastness in which he dwelt. On occasion though, when the seasons ripened the crops in the field, Hans would turn his endeavours in that direction. Although never having been a man of any wealth, Hans remained a proud individual, who would turn his hands to any task in order to provide for his family.

In the same year they built their home in the forest, Brunhilde Krauss, who was a gifted seamstress, had presented her husband with two beautiful daughters. The blonde haired, blue eyed girls were described as angelic by all who set eyes upon them, and to Hans they were the centre of his world.

So life, though humble, was far from wretched for the Krauss family. Hans worked long hours, and Brunhilde looked after the children, while also providing an additional modest income with her sewing talents.

As the twins grew their looks continued to flourish, and so now all who observed the girls described them as being not unlike miniature versions of their mother, for Brunhilde also was a woman of natural beauty. She was known for having the sweetest of dispositions, and with her white blonde hair, stunning blue eyes, and bone structure more suited to a woman of nobler birth; Brunhilde was indeed considered fair by all whose gaze fell upon her.

Some three weeks prior to our having entered this district Hans had turned up in Per, dishevelled and in a distraught condition, crying out for help from anyone learned with medical knowledge. Hans, being a large and powerful man, had arrived in the village having dutifully carried his sick daughter the two leagues from their forest home. Fortune had seemed to be smiling on the doting father, as the good Doctor Haider was already in the village, carrying out a routine treatment on old Mrs Dreher's gout.

Hans' daughter was suffering a strange malaise, and further still seemed to have been hallucinating. She described reoccurring dreams in which mysterious animals visited her, and a beautiful angel would sit by her bed and stroke her hair, before kissing her sweetly on the face and neck.

The doctor, who was from Bruen, two miles south of Per, discerned that the girl's fever was likely attributable to the family's poor living conditions. Nights, even at this time of the year, could turn bitterly cold, and their forest shanty offered scarce protection against the elements. Doctor Haider instructed that the girl, whose name was Lisa, be confined to bed and fed a diet of broth and dumplings, until such time as her fever dropped and she recovered from her lethargy. A number of villagers donated extra blankets, keen that the child's sweats be managed with clean bedding.

Three days later, on a cool and sunny June morning, Hans and Brunhilde Krauss awoke to find the cold, dead body of their daughter strewn across the bed sheets, her face set with an expression of contentment which belied the tragedy of her circumstance. At the time of her death, Lisa had been three months short of her eighth year.

Within three days of burying their child, Brunhilde too had fallen victim to the same malady which had afflicted her daughter. She described dreams of a mysterious woman, who arrived as though stepping from a mist and of how the wraith would sit on her bed and talk attentively of Brunhilde's lost child. On another occasion when the phantom entered the realm of Brunhilde's sleep, she had arrived hand in hand with Lisa. The dead girl no longer looked pallid or weak, as she had been before her death, and she flung her arms about her mother's neck, and the two of them cried tears of joy at their reunion.

Brunhilde was left distraught by the loss of her child; and as such could muster little will to resist the illness which now assailed her. It took little more than a week before she too succumbed to the wrath of this mysterious *fever*.

Now, no one had seen Hans or the remaining girl, whose name was Lara, for almost ten days. Doctor Haider had deferred visiting the Krauss home, lest there be some contagion present, and other locals had also declined venturing to the forest dwelling, for fear of what they may find.

My musing over the recent ills which had afflicted the Krauss family, and other facts which I had discovered during my visit to the inn, were unexpectedly quelled as a howl disrupted the still of the night. The animal was calling its pack-mates with a tone which seemed to suggest, at least to me, a degree of urgency. My first observation being likely borne out as the animals wail was abruptly stifled. There quickly followed a succession of loud yelps and then a shrill scream, followed by another bloodcurdling cry which sounded more animalistic, although this sound did not resemble the pitch offered by a wolf's call.

In barely an instant Rudolph was at my side, pulling off his shirt as he spoke and swiftly discarding it on the ground, "Our brother calls!" his words only confirmed that which I already knew. And then, with a sizeable degree of irritation, "Damn Felix, ever the fool that he is! I told him only to assess our circumstance. I was vehement that he was not to confront these vampires alone."

"And yet he has?" with my question I sought confirmation of the ever more barbarous sounds which were now disrupting the night.

"Indeed, brother. We break now, so keep pace with us as best you can."

I was aware of the hurried pulsation of my veins as all about me my *brothers* pulled at their clothing, hurriedly disposing of these restrictions as they, as one, fell upon all fours. It was their teeth I noted first, their jaws slackening, and then elongating under the flickering of the lantern's shadow-light, now showing sharp, white fangs ready to tear out the beating heart of any unfortunate enough to fall into their path. They ventured forth into the darkness, padding briskly across the forest floor, hair bristling with hate, misshapen creatures the like of which should never have existed. My band of *brothers*, each one a *man* who stands firm and strong, seeming to possess the strength of a giant, but now choosing, allowing with free will the surrender of their souls, to be replaced by the fiendish beast which dwells within each of them.

As the werewolves disappeared into the black of night, the smallest of them twice the size of any wolf I had ever encountered, I set off in swift pursuit. Leastways, as swift a pursuit as a man guided by a solitary lantern can muster when cast adrift amid an ocean of gloom, and where any misplaced step may court tragedy underfoot.

I was closing in on a pinprick of light away in the distance, as I guessed this must be the Krauss residence. It was an assumption based directionally to the sounds of slaughter which now disrupted the night, making a mockery of the previous tranquillity of the forest. I heard, or at least fancied I heard, the high scream of a child, but its resonance hinted of something deeply evil. I slipped and stumbled, falling upon my hands, and my heart sank as I felt the wetness between my fingers. My mind created a vision of the forest floor coated with the blood of innocents, and it was with massive relief that I realised the ground was wet with dew.

I climbed to my feet and carried on running, stumbling and tripping my way towards the light, until finally I burst into a clearing, at the centre of which stood the Krauss home.

The cottage stood as a lone and wretched habitation. Hans Krauss may well have been proficient at bringing down trees, but this miserable construction confirmed the limitations of his talent.

As I moved towards the little home standing in the centre of this sylvan fastness, there was a loud crash and one of the werewolves was dispatched with considerable force through one of the shuttered windows, and landed with an unhealthy *thump* on the ground. At that same moment and for certain my heart gave a great jump, as through the front door of the cottage a great beast emerged. The feline was as black as coal and the size of a leopard, although as it moved across my line of vision I determined its shape and proportional tail length to be more in line with those of a common house cat. Moreover, the animal was moving with considerable speed and, having veered its course, was now headed directly towards me.

I drew my pistol, but as I took aim I realised that two of the wolves had now broken from the house and were bearing down on the cat. Given the speed of their approach, I could not be sure my aim would be true enough to avoid hitting either of my *brothers.*

I holstered the pistol and chose instead to raise my sword, intending to strike with enough violence so as to lop off the black fiend's head. Swiftly the animal was upon me, and it was with a pent up fury that I launched my blow. The cat was faster than I had allowed, and though my aim fell short of true, still I managed to catch the creature forcibly in its shoulder. As the beast was upended it let out a pitiful *mew,* before crashing against the solid base of a pine. The fiend lay dazed, motionless though likely only for a moment, and my heart raced with deep satisfaction as its veil slipped and the revenant resumed the form of a human woman. I gave a shout of delight and stepped forward, raising my sword high, intending to cut off the vampires head!

Then my cry turned to one of despair as I looked down at the naked form of this sallow faced young thing, her arm almost severed at the shoulder as a result of my blow. I lowered my sword and turned my attention towards the Krauss home, leaving my two *brothers* to tear this girl – who was no longer of the living, or a girl - asunder.

As I ran towards the forest hovel my ears were stained by the fearful cries of the revenants demise.

The wolf who had been dispatched through the window was still struggling to find its feet, and upon entering the dwelling I almost lost my own footing, slipping on a floor which was awash with blood. The body of a child lay in the middle of the room, her chest torn open, and her heart devoured, rested as an island amid an ocean of crimson sea.

Three wolves were busying themselves, devouring and disputing over what little remained of another corpse. Once a sizeable man, this was likely what little remained of Hans Krauss.

A female body laid headless, naked and bloodied close by where the wolves were feeding, and just a few feet from here rested her crown, adorned with white blonde hair.

At the far side of the room stood Rudolph, now in human form and stained with the red of victory, he had a gleam of satisfaction in his eyes as he gestured towards the terrified child, wailing and huddled in the corner. "What say you of this one, brother?"

"Is she...?" I asked.

"She is untouched. Though after all she has seen this night it would be kinder to end her now."

"No!"

"She will be forever damaged as a result of these sights," he gestured towards the headless corpse of Brunhilde Krauss, and then at the blood sodden walls and floor of the shack. "For certain, there is but little meat on the child, but still she would make for a tender morsel."

"No!" I rciterated, and I felt my fingers tighten around the handle of my blade. Rudolph could see the look of anger etched on my face, and I don't doubt he delighted in seeing my pain. After all, he has the senses of a wolf; it is obvious he is aware of the distain I hold for him. Although most often I feel that this hunt, and indeed any feeling of disgust he can induce in me, it is all just a part in a larger game which Rudolph chooses to play.

Nonetheless, he nodded agreement. "Very well, brother. Take the child and do as you will with her."

He watched as I scooped the sobbing girl up in my arms, and he smiled a most awful smile as I caressed her hair and attempted, and failed to find some words of comfort.

Rudolph pointed towards where Lisa's body lay, "Soldier Brother, if you are taking this one, then that broken one must be mine," and with that he allowed his body to slip into its lupine form, whereupon he slunk over to Lisa's corpse and began devouring it. I barely managed to avert Lara's eyes and hurry her from the dwelling before the beast commenced its assault on her sister's remains.

As I carried young Lara from the cottage I contemplated the events of recent weeks, and found myself questioning the course of my own actions. Though I attempted to convince myself that God remained by my side, still I would have welcomed the peace of releasing these memories, and surrendering my mind unto a dark fugue.

Chapter 3

Excerpt from the journal of General Spielsdorf, *June 29th,* 1860

The sun was raising high on the eastern horizon by the time the child and I reached the horses, although the night chill had not yet faded under the warmth of the day. I cradled the sleeping girl in a shawl, as I had for most of the night; and the tightness of the grip she applied on my arm only added to the turmoil of the emotions I was experiencing.

It had taken a worryingly short while for sleep to overwhelm the child, and having noted the clamminess and pallor of her skin it occurred to me that, rather than it being a case of exhaustion overcoming her, more likely it was the emotional disturbance of seeing her dead kin rise, only to then be butchered before her eyes. The malady induced by these events may likely have a lasting, and devastating effect.

The horses had been tethered with ample slack, and continued to graze amiably as I approached from the tree-line. Soon my *brothers* would follow out of the forest, once they had carried out their obscene, though necessary, rituals. Their actions would culminate with the burning to the ground of the Krauss home. These were events I had witnessed many times during the previous weeks; I had no stomach for any further viewing.

I approached Marie, a bay mare I had owned for over six years, and that was always my mount of choice. The horse had been bred for military service and was battle-proof when it came to being unsettled.

I had no wish to add to the distress of the child, and so it was with some effort I mounted the horse. I settled the girl in my lap, and then turned my ride southwards. Even in the light of day the land remained flat and uninteresting.

As I headed back across open country, towards the hamlet of Per, my mind drifted to the events of the previous night. More especially to those which had taken place as I floundered through the woods, prior to arriving at the Krauss dwelling.

Felix, in wolf form, had been sent ahead of our party, and had arrived at the cottage to find the door ajar, and from inside the pitiful whimpering sounds of a child. The hovel was well lit, ablaze with fire-light, and the sight which greeted the wolf was one of horror. Brunhilde, her white blonde tresses loosed, was naked on the bed astride her husband. She was a woman of ample pleasures, and the wolf watched as she gyrated astride her man, Hans' nightshirt hoisted around his chest.

Apparently, in lupine form events are often witnessed as though through a fog, but Felix remembered being struck by the silence of their fervour. The woman, though moving as if lost in the throes of passion, remained completely silent. With Hans, too, there was an absence of noise, and throughout their passion he remained deathly still.

Discarded on the floor beside the bed were two funeral gowns. The wolf realised that one belonged to the naked Brunhilde, and quickly it spotted the owner of the other.

At the far side of the room a most dreadful sight greeted its eyes. A sweet faced girl was sitting on a child sized bed, and wailing dreadfully. This girl was precious little Lara, who I now carry to sanctuary. Next to Lara was another child, with the same white blonde hair, but with the face of a demon.

Alongside the bed stood an unhealthily slender, naked woman, with long raven hair. She either heard or sensed the animal's presence, but either way, as she turned to face the wolf its hackles bristled with fear. The fiend looked barely into womanhood, but as she turned for the wolf, she too became possessed by the features of a hellion. Her skin decayed, taking on a rotted, mottled appearance, and her fingers stretched out, lengthening into stiletto talons. The woman's jaw fell open, growing deeper, and displaying a mouthful of barbed, yellowing teeth.

The wolf hurled itself at the slender fiend, its senses identifying her as the greatest threat. However, as it threw itself into the air its attack was stifled by Brunhilde, who with speed belying known reason launched herself off the bed and into the wolfs path. The dead wife succeeded in disrupting the animal's flight, and it crashed with a yelp into the open fire, its tail briefly

25

catching alight. As the wolf yelped in pain, and attempted to roll itself free of the flames, it found itself being gripped by the throat, the slender fiend scooping the animal up and tossing it harshly against the wall of the shack. The infant hellion joined the attack, and it was only the denseness of the animal's fur which prevented the revenants fangs from puncturing flesh. The wolf fought itself free, and as it used its speed to remain elusive within the confines of the wretched hovel, the werewolf called loud for the assistance of his brothers.

The pack arrived swiftly, and the situation descended further into chaos and blood. Seven werewolves and I, matched against three revenants, and one of these a child. Still though, it was to prove a hard fought victory, and one which only began to turn in our favour once Peter, second eldest of the brothers, managed to lock his jaws around Brunhilde's throat. The wolf gnawed, tearing sinew and grinding bone until, finally, it succeeded in parting Brunhilde's head from her neck.

Even following on from this, Lisa had found the strength to fling Karl, the youngest, and by far the one gifted with the most pleasant disposition of any among my *brothers*, clean through the window of the cottage. As the pack members had turned to vent their fury on the child-monster, the slender fiend had grabbed her opportunity, skin-walking into animal form and attempting to make her escape, but, of course, this was the point at which I arrived at the scene.

As I reached the outskirts of Per, my mind once again turned to the cottage the Krauss family had called home. By now it would be fully ablaze, my wolf *brothers* would see to it that no clues remained as to the atrocities which had taken place there.

For the villagers I would present my own version of events, and it was a version likely to be accepted without question. These, like most other country folk, are fearful people. I could tell from my previous visit, there was a worry the Krauss family's illness would spread throughout the community.

I will tell of how my journey north through the forest was halted by the sight of a burning cottage. I shall say that upon investigation I found the stove had been left unattended, and a blaze had caught hold of the building's fragile timbers. Hans Krauss was still in his bed, sick and beyond my help, but I was able to rescue young Lara. Furthermore, I will insist that the girl, though seeming neither sick nor injured by the flames, has a manner which suggests she is in need of urgent care, probably as a result of the fright induced in her by the flames.

The villagers will readily accept this version of events, especially when I tell them I am inclined to pay good coin to Doctor Haider, if he is willing to immediately, and unconditionally arrange the transportation of young Lara, as I would see her re-homed, and educated at the Gratz Friary, home of the Franciscan friars. More importantly, it is the residence of Friar Bauer, a valued friend of my family. He is a kind and just man, whom I have known and trusted since I was a boy.

The people of Per will want the girl moved on, and as soon as is reasonably possible, just perchance she carries the sickness which afflicted her family. Although they would never admit to it, the villagers will be relieved that the possibility of contagion has been cleansed by the fire. Of course, it is not an *infection* of which they would have been contemplative.

As for myself: these events have failed to provide the resolution I sought, but as The Lord God remains my witness, I shall not rest until my quest is completed and I have hunted down and destroyed the monster responsible for my anguish.

An epilogue: less than perfect

Excerpt from the journal of Friar Bauer, *December 4th, 1860*

Today I was witness to a most awful occurrence involving Lara Krauss, the young girl who was orphaned following a house fire which claimed her father, and who was delivered into my care at the behest of my good friend General Spielsdorf.

The day had begun in a harsh manner, but things proceeded to get even worse. Rain, lashed and driven by a north-east wind, had greeted the dawn. By mid-morning even the rain had given up the fight, succumbing to the savagery of a winter storm which took possession of the world like an army of Frost Giants thundering across Bifrost, intent on assailing Asgard's Golden Gates. The early December snow was driven, forming ever deepening blankets of white on the ground, and as it persisted in its fall, the wind too continued to rush about the friary, wrenching at the shutters, battering doors, the gale howling bawdy songs down chimneys, and doing its best to break boughs on the two English Yews which shadow the Main Gates.

The decision had been taken to move the children out of the schoolhouse into the relative comfort of the Main Hall.

The Hall was ablaze with fire-light, and reverberated with the chatter and laughter of the children. Normally the friars would have insisted on the students going quietly about their work, but precious little schooling would be achieved this day. The storm had continued to close in, and even the staff and friars allocated outside duties had now gathered in the Hall, forced to yield to the might of the weather. The Hall was alive with sound, all noisily discussing the ferocity of the storm, and for the youngsters in particular it proved a source of major excitement.

Lunch consisted of freshly baked bread, and bowls of stew, which was brought from the kitchens and distributed among the grateful throng.

The Guardian had already taken the decision to abandon the days schooling, but also to set the keenest children to plaiting wicks for the candles and lamps, items needed if faced with a particularly harsh winter. Those plaiting were sat in circles, each group having a lamp at its centre, and those furthest from the main fire had extra warmth, the back wall lined by four braziers filled with glowing wooden embers. Some of the older orphans were set to replenishing the braziers, as and when required carrying fresh logs from the hearth.

Lara had been set to plaiting, and she was in a group seated close to the main fire. An hour had passed since lunch, when above the noise of the storm we heard knocking at the main door.

Brother Werberg opened the door to admit our unlikely visitor, and as well as being virtually blown off his feet by the strength of the bluster, the friar received a layering of snow which induced howls of hearty laughter amongst the younger children.

Our visitor was Karl Vogl, who entered the Hall along with his German Shepard dog, Basti. Karl was a cooper who ran his business out of a small yard adjacent to the friary. As Brother Werberg battled to close the door against the elements, both man and dog rigorously shook themselves free of their snow trappings. Karl explained that he and Basti, for he always kept the dog by his side wherever he went, had become stranded at his yard. His work hut only had three sides, and as such his brazier had succumbed to the driving snow. Furthermore, the weather was now so fierce he feared attempting the mile to his home, and so came to us seeking sanctuary. It goes without saying, of course, that any man, woman or child would always be made welcome within the walls of our home.

However, even before Karl could warm himself before the fire, a shrill scream echoed around the room. Young Lara Krauss, a girl who has needed coaxing into any form of vocal interaction since her arrival, let out a most awful, and repetitive call. With her eyes locked firmly upon Karl's Shepard dog, "The wolf! The wolf! The wolf! The wolf!" was her terrified cry.

Over and over again the girl screamed her warning, but it wasn't so much the child's wailing which so disturbed those of us in attendance, but rather the level of fear her young voice carried.

Brother Markus was closest to the girl, but his attempts to console her with kind words and reassuring hugs failed beyond measure. Her struggles had grown violent to the point of restraint, and as the girl's shouts grew ever shriller, try as we might we could not comfort her terrors. The dog was swiftly removed to a far chamber, but even then Lara's fear was beyond containable, her body falling into a stiffening spasm. All chatter in the Hall had fallen away leaving a deathly silence, its reign broken only by the distraught sounds emitted by the terrified girl. I clasped my hands and prayed for the girl's salvation, begging The Lord to shine his light on this child's pain.

If I am honest though, panic gripped at my soul as I began to suspect how this tragedy would end, and this even before Lara's heart began to fail her. And as the girl's body sounded its final wheezing death rattle, I fell to my knees and wept.

My friend, The General, had some months earlier saved this poor child's life, and he will surely be distraught when he learns of her fate, especially in light of the recent tragedy which has blighted his own life. When, finally, I am reunited with my old friend, there are questions for which I shall require answers. For never before have I seen a person expire through terror alone, and the girl's age makes it a further travesty. What, pray tell, can this poor child ever have witnessed in her short life which could induce such a fright in her soul?

The mystery unravels, and all will finally be revealed in the pages of Carmilla: The Wolves of Styria.

Preview:

The Moons of Rulan-Ga

On a distant world a young couple plan for their future. Carter and Freya Johns are **lifebound***, and together with other members of Freya's family they take the decision to cross borders, and begin life afresh in the previously sealed Nation-State of Arcadia.*

Carter's mind is troubled by reoccurring dreams of a strange world, a land where the days are warmed by a solitary sol, and whose nights are brightened by a singular moon. Where planes fly through the air, dogs bark in the distance, and people drive strange metallic carriages called cars. Carter has no explanation as to how these things can be so alien and yet also so familiar for him.

Soon though, Carter will forget worrying about this other world, as he realizes an ancient evil has surfaced much closer to home, something dark which lurks among the shadows.

On Earth, Clay Jones leads a solitary existence, constrained by the grief of a tragedy he failed to prevent. So when he is tracked down by a woman asking for help, a desperate mother convinced that Clay is the only man on Earth capable of saving her daughter, Clay is faced with a major decision. Should he keep to his low profile, guilt ridden lifestyle, or should he go up against an evil which has previously bettered him?

Two men, worlds apart, are united in a fight for survival against something less than human.

The teen girl stretched out slender, finely boned limbs, her lips curling to a smile as she felt the coolness of the grass touch her fingers. She shifted, just slightly, and flexed her shoulders against the coarseness of the blanket beneath her. All the while though, she relished the warmth of the late August sun on her body.

In recent years the seasons had proven sporadic, but not this time. A long hard winter had been followed by glorious spring days, which in turn blossomed into one of the warmest summers in decades.

Today, the sun blistered in a pale blue sky, and life seemed good, for everyone.

The hum of traffic was barely audible, the copse, which bordered the grounds of the old house, acting as a useful buffer against the sounds of the main throughway, certainly well enough to distance the property from any noticeable noise pollution.

Over an hour lying out in the sun had dulled the girl's senses to the point where she had become oblivious to almost everything.

She failed to notice the occasional rustle of branches, as they crept through the undergrowth, edging ever closer toward her. Carter though, he knew they were there.

He couldn't yet see them, but he knew he soon would. He listened, waiting for the crack of a branch broken underfoot.

Carter knew that the girl had trodden carelessly, and this in turn caused her sibling a degree of agitation. He knew the boy had halted in his tracks, turning sharply and frowning, a finger pressed to his lips signalling the need for his sister to move with more stealth.

Carter could not see any of this, and yet he knew the girl was nodding apologetically.

The older girl, the one on the blanket, sighed and rolled onto her tummy; she was beginning to feel the burn and maintaining an even tan was of the utmost importance. Carter watched the girl turn; and his mouth curled into a smile as he noted the way her breasts danced inside their leopard print restraint. He knew that her soft, sun pinked flesh interested the boy in the bushes, greatly. And he knew that the boy was unsure as to why such an interest stirred within him.

Somewhere far away a dog had begun to bark, but the sound offered barely a whispered annoyance before being carried away on rising currents of warm air.

Carter watched the children as they edged clear of the foliage. He saw the girl deliver a sharp dig to the ribs of her brother, and indicate to him she had disengaged the safety on her weapon. The boy nodded sternly and flipped the catch on his own pistol, before sliding his finger onto the trigger.

The blanket girl opened her mouth to scream, but instead found herself sucking in a sharp intake of breath, the force of the initial impact temporarily silencing her vocal chords. But then, as she touched her hand to the wetness on her back, she found her voice and let out a yell of shocked indignation.

Her assailants chose to ignore her pleas for clemency, and instead unleashed the full fury of the firepower at their disposal. The two children squealed with delight at the sight of their victim attempting to gain a foothold, rejoicing at seeing her pegged back by the force of the water expelled from their Blitz cannons.

They were still yelling fits of laughter as they threw their weapons to the ground and turned to flee, heading towards the sanctity of the main house with the older girl's threats of violent retribution rattling their ears. But neither cared, choosing rather to relish the glorious victory of their surprise assault.

Their pursuer let out a cry of delight as she realized one of the discarded cannons still contained a quantity of water, and snatching up the toy she set off in hasty pursuit.

As the siblings raced onto the closely mown slope leading up and away from the main garden, Carter grimaced as he recognized their intention to seek sanctuary inside the house. The children had realized the older girl would have to refrain from using the cannon once they were ensconced inside, and they squawked with delight as they saw her slip, wet feet betraying her to the sloping lawn.

But Carter's eyes were already focused on the house.

The three-storied red brick had a deep front porch, with a swing and a pair of rocking chairs positioned either side of the main entrance.

With the sun having begun its eastward descent a partial shadow now fell on the veranda, blackening windows and darkening the features of the cushioned rockers.

Beyond the children, Carter spied movement. He stared intently toward the terrace, as from out of the dulling greyness - something darker formed.

Carter strained his eyes, desperate this time to try and make out more of the detail – as black as ink and yet possessing no more substance than the shadows from which it came. The form, at least briefly, resembled the figure of a man. However, as Carter watched, the shadow-man melted into a swirling, serpentine mass of fluctuating dark. Quickly, yet with a stealth belying any mirage, the darkness moved, slithering rapidly over the decking and through the open front door, before disappearing into the gloom of the house.

Carter was gripped by a rising tide of terror, and he screamed a warning to the children, crying out to them that they should stay away from the building. Instead, they ran up onto the porch, turned briefly to mock the chasing girl, and disappeared inside. As was ever the case, they had neither seen nor heard Carter.

Carter turned in his sleep and his eyelids twitched, then opened with a start. His eyes were fixed on the ribbed vault ceiling; edged with an armature of piped masonry, but no thoughts were lost to the splendour of his surroundings, only dream-thoughts tumbled through his head – stumbling over themselves to disperse before he might rationalize them. Beads of sweat dampened his body, and, as always, it was the same questions which troubled these waking moments.

The unusual design of the house in the dream? Weapons which dispensed water? Dogs? Traffic? A solitary sol in the sky? Each of these things and words were of a nature unknown to Carter, and yet also seemed vaguely familiar.

These same images now disturbed him far too frequently, and he shuddered as thoughts of the shadow-man returned to him. He rolled onto his side, choosing to turn his attention to the aesthetic features of the woman sleeping beside him, and allowing his troubled dreams to disperse into the ether.

The day was still in its infancy, and yet already the sols' were creeping over the horizon. Overhead a flow of Raliens avers were *caw-cawing* their way across the first light. At this time the downs would still be damping, and a plentiful surfacing of wrigglers would guarantee the attention of numerous varieties of avers, but the heavier set Raliens would, as always, bully themselves onto the prime feeding pits.

The Raliens cry was one recognised throughout Calibrue, and to Carter it heralded the glorious birth and timely death of each day.

In the courtyard below stable hands were busying themselves harnessing a team of dulons, the animals snorting indignation under the weight of their shackles. The gruff tones of Ramol Gruen now rose above the throng, issuing instructions to various staff, and urging them to carry out their tasks with more haste. Ramol was a man who would leave nothing to chance, and although ensuring the animals were correctly harnessed, and the carriage fully laden with supplies was not of his remit, the guard would take no chances when it came to the wellbeing of the former Minister Prime.

Carter's mind returned briefly to the dream, but he dispelled these thoughts in favour of pondering the vagaries of his own beginnings. Then, as he turned once more to admire the features of his lifebound, he considered the coming hardship of the journey upon which they were about to embark, and he realized that, for reasons which eluded him, an icy chill had begun to run the length of his spine.

The Moons of Rulan-Ga will be available in 2014.

A footnote regarding *Carmilla: A Dark Fugue*: Geography students and residents of Austria may realize I have taken certain geographical liberties. What can I say? It was just how the story mapped out (do you see what I did there?).

Made in the USA
Coppell, TX
19 January 2023